PETER PAN

TREASURY OF ILLUSTRATED CLASSICS™

PETER PAN

by
J. M. Barrie
[Sir James Matthew Barrie]

**Abridged, adapted,
& illustrated**
by
quadrum■

Modern Publishing
A Division of Kappa Books Publishers, LLC.

Cover art by Marcel Laverdet

Contents

Chapter 1

Peter Breaks Through

The Darling family lived in London. Wendy was the oldest of the Darling children. John followed her, while Michael was the youngest. When she was younger, Wendy would often think that her parents would give her away, as there were too many mouths to feed. Her father was extremely proud of her, but he never showed it.

The family had a dog, a Newfoundland called Nana. They trusted her with their lives. Nana was their appointed nurse for the kids. All in all, the Darlings were the simplest, happiest family in London, until Peter Pan came.

The Darling children often thought of Neverland, which was

more or less an island with vibrant colors and clear water surrounding the island with coral reefs. Peter Pan lived here with Tinker Bell, a tiny fairy.

For each child, Neverland had something different. John, for instance, had flamingos in his Neverland, which would fly over a lagoon while he shot at them. Michael, who was small, had a flamingo with lagoons flying over it in his mind. John lived in a boat turned upside down on the sands, Michael in a wigwam, Wendy in a house of leaves deftly sewn together.

Occasionally Mrs. Darling would question them about Peter Pan. She knew nothing of him, yet he was always there in the minds of her children. When Wendy was questioned about him, she sadly admitted that he was strange.

"But, my pet, who is he?" asked Mrs. Darling.

"Peter Pan, Mother," replied Wendy.

"He hasn't grown up at all! He's just my size." Wendy said this with a lot of confidence, like she knew it for a fact.

When Mrs. Darling told her husband about this, he just laughed it off and told her to leave the children to their imagination. "It will all go away," he assured her.

But it didn't, and soon Peter Pan gave Mrs. Darling quite a shock. Quite often, she would find dry leaves in the nursery that weren't there when she put the children to sleep. There were also muddy footprints on the floor. Wendy just shook her head and smiled at this. "It's Peter again."

"What do you mean, Wendy?"

"He never wipes his feet." Wendy sighed.

She explained frankly to her mother that she thought Peter

sometimes came into the nursery, sat at the foot of her bed, and played his pipes for her. Somehow, she was always asleep and even though she didn't see him while awake, she knew it was him.

"What nonsense! No one can get into the house without knocking," argued Mrs. Darling.

"Mother, he uses the window."

"The nursery window is three floors up, Wendy." Later she found dry leaves near the window. Wendy found this natural, and Mrs. Darling found it hard to dismiss.

The very next night, the lives of Wendy and her brothers were going to change forever.

Chapter 2

Come Away, Come Away!

The next night, Mr. and Mrs. Darling went out to a dinner party. The Darling children wanted to stay awake when Peter arrived, but somehow they always fell fast asleep before he did. Later that night, while the children slept,

Nana walked in to check on them. She saw a strange boy entering through the window, so she growled and jumped on him. He leaped lightly out, through the window. As he reached forward to pull the windows shut, he saw something hanging from Nana's mouth. It was his shadow!

After Nana left the room, a tiny glowing light flew inside quickly. It went inside cupboards and drawers, as if looking for Peter's shadow. The moving light was actually a tiny fairy called Tinker Bell.

A minute after she entered, the windows burst open and Peter flew in. "Tinker Bell!" he called out to her softly, so that the children wouldn't wake up. "Tink, where are you?"

"Tink, tell me where they've put my shadow!"

The loveliest tinkle, like that of golden bells, answered him. It was fairy language. She told him that the shadow was in the chest of drawers. Peter went to the chest immediately, scattering its contents

on the floor. Tinker Bell entered the drawer to help him. When he finally found his shadow, he was so happy that he shut the drawer with Tinker Bell in it.

Peter went to the bathroom and tried sticking his shadow back on by using soap. When the shadow kept slipping off, he sat on the floor and began to cry. His sobs woke Wendy up.

"Boy, why are you crying?" she asked.

In response, Peter stood on his feet and bowed beautifully as a mark of courtesy to her. She was so pleased that, from her bed, she curtsied equally well.

"What's your name?" he asked.

"Wendy Moira Angela Darling. What's your name?"

"Peter Pan."

"Is that all?"

"Yes," he replied sharply, realizing how short his name was next to her name. When she asked where he lived, he told her that he lived on the second star to the right, and straight on till morning.

"That's a funny address!" she replied.

"It is not!" he countered back.

"Do you have a mother?" she asked. He remained silent and lowered his head. "Oh dear, no wonder you've been crying." She climbed off her bed and went to him.

"I wasn't crying because I don't have a mother. I was crying because I couldn't get my shadow to stick," Peter said.

"It has to be sewn on. I'll do it for you," said Wendy.

As she sewed the shadow back on, she noticed that he was clenching his teeth because of the pain. Once she was done, he jumped around the room with joy. Unfortunately,

he forgot to give Wendy the credit, and thought that he had sewed the shadow back on himself.

"How clever I am!" he crowed rapturously. "Oh, the cleverness of me!"

Wendy was shocked. Peter said, "Wendy, I can't help being

this way when I'm happy. One girl is always more useful than twenty boys, you know."

"Do you really think so?" she asked, and Peter solemnly nodded. Wendy happily got out of bed and told him that she would give him a kiss. But Peter didn't know what a kiss was, so he held out his hand to receive it.

"Don't you know what a kiss is?" Wendy asked, shocked.

"I'll know when you give it to me," Peter replied stiffly. She gave him a thimble so that his feelings wouldn't get hurt.

"May I kiss you now?" Peter asked Wendy.

"If you like," she replied primly, slowly inclining her face toward his.

But Peter just dropped an acorn button into her hand. Blushing slightly, she thanked him and put the acorn button around the chain she wore. It was lucky she did, for that very acorn button turned out to save her life later on.

"How old are you?" Wendy asked Peter.

"I don't know exactly. But I am young," he said. "I ran away from home to look for fairies the day I was born."

"But some of us don't believe in fairies anymore," Wendy said, gravely.

"Don't say that!" Peter cried. "Each time you say something like not believing in fairies, somewhere, a fairy drops dead!" He got up and called out for Tinker Bell.

"Peter! Is there a fairy in this room?" Wendy asked.

"She was here, can you hear her?"

"Only the sound of tinkling bells."

"That, Wendy, is the language of the fairies," Peter said.

He noticed the sound was coming from the chest of drawers. He laughed.

"I think I've locked her in there, by mistake."

After he let the poor fairy out, she flew all over him, making agitated signs with her hands. "Now, Tink, don't say that. I didn't mean to lock you in there!"

"Peter, I would like to see her.

Can she hold still?" cried Wendy.

When Tinker Bell finally settled on top of a table, Wendy gushed on how beautiful the fairy was.

"Tink," said Peter amiably, "this lady says she wishes you were her fairy."

Tinker Bell shook her head

insolently.

"What does she say, Peter?" asked Wendy.

Peter had to translate. "She is not very polite. She says you are an ugly girl, and that she is my fairy."

Wendy sat down on an armchair and asked Peter whom he lived with. He told her he lived with the Lost Boys.

"Who are they?" she asked.

"They are those children whose nurses lose them when they are babies. If not found in a week, they are sent to Neverland. I'm their captain," declared Peter. Wendy asked if there were any girls there. "No, girls are too clever to fall out of prams," said Peter.

"I think," Wendy said, "it is

perfectly lovely the way you
about girls; John there just hates
girls." In reply, Peter rose and kicked
John out of bed, blankets and all, in
one kick. John and Michael got up.
Hearing all the noise in the nursery,
Mrs. Darling came in to check. It
was dark in the nursery, and the

behind the curtains
...elic breathing sounds
...hey were asleep. Mrs.
Da...ought it was Nana who
was being naughty. She woke Mr.
Darling, who went and tied poor
Nana up in the kennel.

After they had left, Wendy
asked Peter if he came every night.
She was mildly disappointed to
find out that he came to hear her
stories, not to see her. Just then,
Peter grabbed her hand and started
pulling her toward the window.

"Peter, let me go!" she cried.

"Come back with me! You can
tell the Lost Boys some of your
stories," he pleaded.

"But, I can't!" said Wendy sadly.
"I don't even know how to fly!"

"I'll teach you."

How could she resist. "Of course, it's awfully fascinating!" she said. "Peter, would you teach John and Michael to fly, too?"

He nodded, so Wendy happily asked John and Michael if they would also like to learn how to fly.

"I say, Peter, can you really fly?" asked John, putting on his glasses.

Instead of answering him, Peter flew around the room, taking

the mantelpiece on the way.

Both John and Michael clapped their hands with glee. They asked how they could fly. Peter grabbed some fairy dust from Tinker Bell and blew it all over them. He then told them to think happy thoughts.

They closed their eyes and thought of their happiest memory. When they opened their eyes again, they were airborne!

They all cried out their joy and shock, "Look at me!" "I'm flying!"

"I'll be taking you to a land where there are mermaids—"

"Mermaids!" cried Wendy.

"—and pirates!" said Peter.

"Pirates!" cried John and Michael. "Let's go!" they all cried.

Led by Tinker Bell and Peter,

the three Darling children went out
flying through the window into the
twinkling stars!

Chapter 3

The Flight

To go to Neverland, the children had to go to the second star on the right, and straight on till morning. Peter Pan's companions trusted him and followed him wherever he flew. The trouble was, at this hour of the night, the Darling children were sleepy, and if any one of them dozed off, he or she would drop to the ground like a stone! What was worse, Peter found this hilarious. After all, he could sleep in the air without falling.

"Be nice to Peter! What if he leaves us?" Wendy told her two

little brothers.

"We could go back," Michael said happily.

"How could we ever find our way back without him?"

"Well, then, we could go on," said John.

"That is the awful thing, John. We just have to go on, for we don't know how to stop."

It was true, for Peter had

forgotten to show them how to stop. John told them that if worst came to worst, they should just fly straight ahead. Since the world was round, they'd come back to London eventually.

After flying on for what seemed like hours, he cried out, "We get off here!"

"Where, where?"

"Where all the arrows are pointing."

They saw millions of golden arrows pointing out to an island, guided by the Sun, who wanted to make sure the children didn't get lost, before he retired for the night.

As they saw the island, the children were shocked; for this was the same island they had dreamt about every night!

"John, there's the lagoon!" cried Wendy. "I see your flamingo with the broken leg!"

"Michael, there's your cave!"

"Wendy, there is your wolf with her cubs! In the bushes!"

"John, I see smoke over the Redskin camp," said Wendy.

All this time, Peter grew annoyed that they knew so much about his island. As he guided them lower, he whispered to John, "Would you like to have an adventure, John? Or would you like to have your tea first?"

John hesitated. "What kind of adventure?" he asked cautiously.

"There's a pirate asleep in the

pampas just beneath us," Peter told him.

"If you like, we'll go down and kill him."

"I don't see him," John said after a long pause.

"I do."

"What if he woke up?"

"I only kill them when they are awake, not while they sleep!" Peter replied indignantly. John asked Peter who the pirate captain was.

"Hook," said Peter, with a look of hatred on his face.

Michael began to cry, and even John could speak in gulps only, for they knew Hook's reputation.

"He is the worst of them all. He is the only man of whom the famous dreadful pirate Long John

Silver was afraid."

"What is he like? Is he big?" John asked.

"He is not as big as he was."

"How do you mean?"

"I cut off a bit of him—his right hand. He wears an iron hook in place of it," said Peter. "John, I want you to promise me. If we meet Hook in a fight, you leave him to me."

"I promise," said John loyally. Just then, Tinker Bell fluttered around Peter. He told the others that they had been spotted by the pirates. "They saw Tink's light."

"Tell her to go away at once, Peter," the three cried at once, but Peter refused.

"She's frightened, too. I can't

send her away."

"Then tell her to put her light

out," begged Wendy.

"She can't put it out. That is about the only thing fairies can't do. It just goes out itself when she falls asleep."

"Then tell her to sleep at once," John almost ordered. "She can't sleep except when she's sleepy. It is the only other thing fairies can't do." Peter grabbed John's hat and put Tinker Bell there, the cover of the black top hat covering her glow completely. As they were flying, the air suddenly shook with a tremendous blast. The pirates had fired cannon at them! Luckily no one got hit! But Peter had been carried by the wind of the shot far out to sea, while Wendy was blown upward with no one but Tinker Bell.

Tinker Bell had waited for this moment. She flew out of the hat and got Wendy to follow her. What else could poor Wendy do? She called to Peter, John, and Michael, and got only mocking echoes in reply. Wendy did not yet know that Tink was jealous of Wendy and hated her fiercely. And now, staggering in her flight, she followed Tink to her doom.

Chapter 4

The Island Come True

Neverland buzzed to life upon Peter's arrival. By that evening, the Lost Boys came out to look for Peter; the pirates came out looking for the Lost Boys; the Redskins were looking for the pirates; the beasts were looking for the Redskins.

They were all over the island. All of them wanted blood, except the Lost Boys, who just wanted to find their captain.

The Lost Boys wore animal skins. There were six of them in all. There were Tootles, Nibs, Slightly, Curly, and the Twins. Just as the Lost Boys disappeared, the pirates filled their place.

There was the handsome Italian Cecco, the tattooed Billy Jukes, Cookson, Gentleman Starkey, Noodler, Rob Mullins, Alf Mason, and Irishman Smee.

Finally there was Captain James Hook himself. In person, he was absolutely deathly looking

and dark faced. His hair was in long, black curls. He had beautiful, soulful blue eyes that turned hard when he was sticking his hook through someone.

As the pirates went on their way, the Redskins followed, each of them alert.

They carried tomahawks and knives, and their naked bodies gleamed with paint and oil. Strung around them were scalps of boys as well as of pirates. These were of the Piccaninny tribe.

Leading them was Great Big Little Panther, the Redskin with so many scalps that they got in his way all the time. Lastly, there was the fearless Tiger Lily. She was the most beautiful of her kind, stylish, courageous, and cold and loving when required. As they walked they hardly made a sound, even when they stepped over dry wood. The only sound that was heard was their breathing.

Once the Redskins disappeared, the beasts came out of hiding: lions, tigers, bears, and every kind of beast, mostly the

man-eaters. Their tongues were hanging out; they were hungry to-night. After they passed came the last figure of all, a gigantic, hungry-looking crocodile.

The Lost Boys came close to their underground home. "I do wish Peter would come back," they said nervously, even though in height and breadth they were all larger than their captain.

Just then, Nibs rushed breathless into their midst, pursued by a pack of wolves. The boys quickly gathered around him and made dreadful faces, scaring the wolves away.

Suddenly, they heard a sound and they all scampered back into their hideout. It was the pirates.

Captain Hook told his men
to spread out. As they walked in
different directions, Hook told Smee
how much he wanted Peter. "That

boy cut off my arm and fed it to the crocodile! He will pay dearly for it."

"Smee," Hook went on huskily, "that crocodile would have had me before this, but by a lucky chance it swallowed a clock that goes tick-tick inside it, and so before it can reach me, I hear the tick and run."

He laughed, but in a hollow way.

"Someday," said Smee, "the clock will run down, and then he'll get you."

Hook wetted his dry lips. "Yeah," he said, "that's the fear that haunts me."

Just then, they noticed a rather large mushroom on the ground. When they pulled it out with some effort, they saw that it blocked an opening from which a lot of smoke was coming out. The pirates looked at each other.

"A chimney!" they both exclaimed.

It was indeed a chimney, one that belonged to the underground home of the Lost Boys and Peter

Pan. The boys always blocked it with a mushroom whenever the enemies were nearby.

Along with smoke, their voices were heard, loud and clear, for they had no fear while in their underground hideout. The pirates listened for a while, and then replaced the mushroom, noticing some holes on seven trees.

"Did you hear them say Peter Pan's come home?" Smee whispered excitedly.

Just then, the captain heard a tick-tick in the distance. The sound became crystal clear as it came closer.

"The crocodile!" Hook cried, and bolted, hurriedly followed by Smee.

The Lost Boys came out of hiding and, at that moment, looked up into the sky.

"A great white bird. It is flying this way," cried Nibs.

"What kind of bird?" asked the other boys.

"I don't know," Nibs said, awestruck, "but it looks so weary, and as it flies, it moans, 'Poor Wendy.'"

"Poor Wendy?"

"I remember," said Slightly instantly, "there are birds called Wendies."

"See, it comes!" cried Curly, pointing to Wendy in the skies. Just then Tinker Bell appeared before them and told them that Peter wanted them to shoot Wendy.

Not used to disobeying Peter, Tootles quickly fitted an arrow to his bow. "Out of the way, Tink," he shouted, and then he fired, and Wendy fluttered to the ground with an arrow in her breast.

Chapter 5

The Little House and a Home Under the Ground!

Tootles stood like a conqueror over Wendy's body when the others ran from the trees. "You are all late. I've shot Wendy! Peter will be so proud of me," he shouted.

Slightly was the first to speak. "This is no bird," he said in a scared voice. "I think this must be a lady, and I think we killed her." Tootles, his mouth open with shock, began to tremble. The Boys took off their caps.

"Peter was bringing her to us! And you killed her," said Curly.

"A lady to take care of us at last,"

said one of the Twins, "and now she's gone." Tootles was ashamed now and started walking away. "Come back!" the others cried.

"I can't. I'm too afraid of Peter."

At that moment, they all heard a sound that brought fear to their hearts: Peter's crowing. "Peter!" they cried, for he always signaled his return in this manner.

"Hide her," they whispered, and gathered hastily around Wendy, but Tootles stood aloof. A second later, Peter dropped to the ground.

"Greetings, boys!" he cried, smiling. The boys saluted, but didn't seem as excited. Peter frowned. "I am back," he said hotly. "Why do you not cheer?" Before he gave them a chance to reply, he quickly told them excitedly that he had brought along a mother to look after them.

"Have you not seen her?" asked Peter. "She flew this way."

"Peter," Tootles said quietly, "I will show her to you," and when the others would still have hidden her, he said, "Back, Twins. Let Peter

see."

They all stood back and let Peter have a look at her. Peter noticed the arrow that had struck her. He picked it up.

"Whose arrow is this?" he growled.

"Mine, Peter," said Tootles, who had gone down on his knees.

As Peter was about to strike him with the arrow, Wendy's arm moved. "She lives," Peter said briefly.

When Peter knelt beside her, he noticed that the arrow had pierced the acorn button he had given her, which she had tied to the chain around her neck. As he tried to revive her, he heard an awful wailing.

"That's Tink," said Curly. "She's crying because Wendy lives." Then the boys told them about Tinker Bell and what she made them do, and they never saw him looking angrier. He got to his feet and yelled at the top of his voice, "Tinker Bell! Listen to me. I'm no longer your friend. Be gone forever!"

Tinker Bell rushed and tugged his shoulder, pleading for forgiveness, but he kept brushing her off. Only when he saw Wendy moving slightly did he say, "Not forever, but for a whole week!"

After she flew away, Peter ordered the boys to build a house around Wendy, as it would be very ungentlemanly to pick her up; she was, after all, a lady.

The boys hurriedly went to build the best house for their lady. As they were leaving, John and Michael appeared. When they saw Wendy on the ground, they asked Peter if she was sleeping. When Peter replied that she was and that he and the Lost Boys were building a house for her, John said snobbishly, "Whatever

for? She's just a girl."

"That," explained Curly, "is why we are her servants."

"You? Wendy's servants!"

"Yes," said Peter, "and you also. Away with them."

The surprised brothers were dragged away to work and toil. After a long time, one of the boys came to check on Wendy. He cried out, "She's moving, Peter!" By the time she woke up fully, the house was completely ready.

"Where am I?" Wendy asked.

"Lady, we built this house for you!" Slightly said proudly.

"What a lovely, darling house," Wendy said, and they were the very words the boys had hoped she would say.

"And we're your children!" said the Twins.

With that, the boys went on their knees with their arms outstretched. "Oh, Wendy, please be our mother!"

"But I am only a little girl. I have no real experience," Wendy said, taken aback.

"It doesn't matter. All we need is a nice motherly person," said Peter.

"Well, I know I am that!" smiled Wendy.

"We know!" cried the Lost Boys. "We saw that at once!"

"Very well," she said, "I will do my best. Come inside at once; before I put you to bed, I have just enough time to finish the story of Cinderella." So in they all went, except Peter, who stood outside to guard the place.

After a while, he started falling asleep, and some little fairies came and played about near him.

Wendy was being a very good mother. The wicked pirates had slyly baked a poisonous cake for the boys. But Wendy snatched it away before anyone could eat even a bite, and saved the boys.

One of the first things Peter did the next day was to measure Wendy,

John, and Michael for hollow trees. Wendy and Michael fitted their trees at the first try, but John had to be altered a little. They grew to love their home under the ground; especially Wendy.

Peter, along with Wendy, invented a new game that did not involve adventures, like sitting on stools, flinging balls in the air, pushing one another, etc. To see Peter sitting doing nothing on a

stool was a great sight.

Imagination and make-believe played a very important role in Peter's and his friend's lives. It was so powerful, so real, that even if there was nothing on a plate, all you had to do was make-believe that your plate was filled with things to eat!

Wendy's favorite pastime was sewing and darning, after the entire household was asleep. She spent the free time she had in making new clothes for the boys.

The pet wolf Wendy had dreamt of very soon discovered that she was on the island and it followed her everywhere.

Chapter 6

The Mermaids' Lagoon

The children often spent long summer days on the lagoon, swimming or floating most of the time, playing the mermaid game in the water. But that didn't mean that the mermaids were friendly.

Often, Wendy would go to the edge of Marooners' Rock so that she could see the mermaids basking in the sun and combing their long hair. If ever she was in the water, they would splash water all over her with their tails, intentionally. They even treated the boys the same way, all except Peter. They would chat with Peter for hours on Marooners' Rock.

But the lagoon was as dangerous in the night as it was

beautiful in the morning. The moment the moon rose, one heard haunting wails coming from the depths.

During the day, the mermaids played their games with bubbles made with the colors of the rainbow. John introduced a new way of hitting the bubble, with the head instead of the hand, and the mermaids quickly adopted it. This was the one mark that John left on Neverland.

One fateful night, at the Marooners' Rock, Peter stood still, cocking his ears from this way to that. His eyes widened.

"Pirates! They are coming this way!" he whispered harshly. He signaled the boys awake. A strange smile was playing about his face—Wendy saw it and shuddered. While that smile was on his face, no one dared address him; all they could do was to stand ready to obey. The order came sharply.

"Dive!"

Within a second, the lagoon seemed deserted. A boat drew close. In the boat were Smee, Starkey, and their Redskin captive, Tiger Lily! They had tied her hands and ankles. The two pirates did not see the rock till they crashed straight into it.

"Luff, you lubber," cried an Irish voice that was Smee's. "Here's the rock. Now, then, what we have to do is to hoist the Redskin onto it, and leave her here to drown."

Behind the rock, Wendy and Peter saw the entire incident. Wendy started crying, as this was the very first tragedy she had ever seen. But Peter paid her no heed; he was worried about Tiger Lily. He knew he had to save her!

He quickly imitated the voice of Captain Hook.

"Ahoy there, you lubbers!" he called. It was a marvelous imitation.

"The captain?!" said the pirates,

staring at one another in surprise. "We have put the Redskin on the rock," Smee called out.

"Set her free," came the astonishing answer.

"Free?!"

"Yes, cut her bonds and let her go."

"But, Captain—"

"At once, do you hear," cried Peter, "or I'll plunge my hook into the two of you."

"Better do what the captain orders," said Starkey nervously.

"Ay, ay," Smee said, and he cut Tiger Lily's cords. At once, like an eel, she slid between Starkey's legs into the water.

"Boat ahoy!" came a voice, but this time it was not Peter who had spoken. Now Wendy understood. The real Hook was also in the water. He was swimming toward the boat, guided by the lamp of the lantern with one of his men.

"Captain, is all well?" they asked timidly, but he answered with a hollow moan. Then, at last, he spoke passionately. "The game's up," he cried. "Those boys have found a mother."

"What's a mother?" asked the ignorant Smee. Wendy was so shocked that she exclaimed, "He doesn't know!"

Peter pulled her beneath the water, for Hook had become alert, and cried, "What was that?"

"I heard nothing," said Starkey, raising the lantern over the waters, and as the pirates looked, they saw a strange sight. There was a nest floating on the river, with a Never Bird in it.

"See," said Hook in answer to Smee's question, "that is a mother. What a lesson! The nest must have fallen into the water, but would the mother desert her eggs? No."

"Captain," said Smee, "could we not kidnap the boys' mother and make her our mother?"

"Brilliant idea!" cried Hook. "We will seize the children and carry them to the boat. The boys we will make walk the plank, and Wendy shall be our mother."

They all agreed. Suddenly, Hook remembered Tiger Lily. "Where is the captured Redskin?"

he demanded abruptly.

His men thought he still was in a playful mood. "We let her go, just like you told us to," giggled Smee.

"Let her go?"

"You told us to!" the pirates argued.

"Rubbish!" cried Hook. "I've given no such orders!"

"Blimey, this is all strange," muttered Smee.

Hook looked around the lagoon. "Spirits that haunt the lagoon tonight, can you hear me?"

Peter, even though he should have kept quiet, answered Hook: "Aye, I hear ye."

Hook didn't even pale. "Who are you?" he shouted.

"I am James Hook, Captain

of the *Jolly Roger!*" the voice
rang back. "And you are just
a codfish!"

Hook gulped once or twice and
tried to guess who was speaking.
"Do you have another voice?"

Peter, who could never resist

a game, replied in his own voice, "I do."

"Boy?"

"Yes."

"Ordinary boy?"

"No!"

"Wonderful boy?"

"Yes."

"Are you in England?"

"No."

"Are you here?"

"Yes."

Hook was completely puzzled. "You ask him some questions," he said to the others, wiping his damp brow.

Smee reflected. "I can't think of a thing," he said regretfully.

"Can't guess, can't guess!" crowed Peter. "Do you give it up?"

Of course, in his pride, he was carrying the game too far, and the villains saw their chance. "Yes, yes," they answered eagerly.

"Well, then," he cried excitedly, "I am Peter Pan."

"Now we know who the mischief-maker is and we will soon have him!" Hook shouted. "Into the water, Smee. Starkey, mind the boat. Take Peter Pan dead or alive!"

The fight was short and gallant. While the Lost Boys went after Smee and Starkey, Peter went for Hook. Hook had climbed up a rock to catch some air, and Peter flew to meet him. He saw that he was higher up the rock than his foe. It would not have been fighting fair.

He gave Hook a hand to help him up.

It was then that Hook bit him. What stunned Peter was not the pain, but the unfairness at which he got bitten. A few minutes later, however, the Lost Boys saw Hook swimming away in the water, a look of pure terror on his face. The hungry crocodile, which had appeared tick-ticking just in time, chased him stealthily.

The boys were worried about Peter and Wendy, whom they couldn't find. They began searching around the lagoon for them.

Suddenly, they saw Wendy slumped against a weak Peter on a small rock, which would soon be underwater. Just then, something

light brushed against Peter's cheek. It was the tail of a kite that Michael made a few days earlier. Peter looked at it and, the next instant, he grabbed the tail of the kite and pulled it to him.

"It lifted Michael off the ground," he cried. "Why should it not carry you?"

"Both of us!" Wendy wondered.

"It can't lift two; Michael and Curly tried. Let us draw lots."

"Ladies first, I say," said Peter softly as he tied the kite's tail around her waist. She clung to him and refused to go without him; but with a "Good-bye, Wendy," he pushed her from the rock, and in a few minutes she was borne out of his sight. Peter was alone on the lagoon.

For a moment he felt a tremor of fear and nervousness go through him as he stood alone in the lagoon, on the rock. Next moment he was standing erect on the rock again, with that smile on his face and a drum beating within him. It was saying, "To die will be an awfully big adventure."

Chapter 7

The Never Bird

The last sound that Peter heard before he was truly alone was that of mermaids retiring to their underwater chambers. Once the waters settled again, his attention went to something floating in the lagoon. It was the Never Bird, making desperate efforts to reach

Peter on the nest. She had come to save him, to give him her nest, though there were eggs in it.

Neither of them understood the other's language. Nevertheless, the bird managed to get her nest to him, and then she flew away, making room for him with her eggs. She looked down, hoping he'd understand her. It took him a moment, but he did. She saw him climb into the nest and examine her eggs. She covered her eyes with her wings, but she couldn't help looking between the feathers.

He took out her eggs and placed them on his hat. They floated rather well. Relieved, the Never Bird flew to her eggs and snuggled herself over them.

She drifted in one direction, and he was borne off in another, both cheering.

The Lost Boys rejoiced the return of their captain in their underground home. Peter came back around the same time Wendy did, who was taken for a joy ride by the kite. But Wendy, though happy to have them all home again, safe and sound, was bothered by the lateness of the hour, and cried,

"To bed, to bed," in a voice that had to be obeyed. Next day, however, she was awfully tender, and gave out bandages to everyone who was hurt.

The Boys played till bedtime, pretending to limp about and carrying their arms in false

slings.

Chapter 8

The Happy Home

The Redskins became Peter's
friends as he had saved Tiger Lily
from a dreadful fate. She and her

tribe owed their lives to him. All night they sat around Peter's home, keeping guard. During the day they'd smoke their pipe of peace. They called Peter the Great White Father. Each time he appeared before them, they'd bow down on their knees, which pleased Peter immensely.

"The Great White Father," he would say to them in a very lordly manner as they groveled at his feet, "is glad to see the Piccaninny warriors protecting his wigwam from the pirates."

"Me Tiger Lily," the lovely Redskin would say. "Peter Pan save me, me his velly nice friend. Me no let Pirates hurt him."

Even Wendy was very happy.

After the meals, she would tell
the boys to clear away the dining
table. She would then sit down
to her work-basket with a heavy
load of stockings to mend—almost
every knee would have a hole

in it.

As she sewed, she would watch the boys playing with one another. This had become such a common scene, a scene she had grown to love. She would hear a sharp step above her and tell the boys that Peter would like them to meet him upstairs.

Peter would bring nuts for the boys as well as the correct time for Wendy.

"Peter, you just spoil them, you know," Wendy would say with a warm smile.

One day, the first Twin came to Peter. "Father, we want to dance."

"Dance away, my little man," said Peter, who was in a merry mood.

"But we want you to dance."

Peter was really the best dancer among them, but he pretended to be scandalized.

"Me! My old bones would rattle!" he cried.

"And Mother, too."

"What," cried Wendy. "The mother of such an armful, dance!"

Wendy told the boys that she would dance only after they get into their nighties. Peter sat down with her near the fire and said, "There is nothing more I like than to spend my evenings with you by the fire after a hard day's work, with the little ones at my feet."

She went to him and put her hand on his shoulder.

"Dear Peter," she said, "with

such a large family, of course, I have now become old and tired, but you don't want to change me, do you?"

"No, Wendy." And he fell silent after that.

"Peter what is it?" asked Wendy after a while.

"This is all just make-believe, right? Me 'being' their father?"

"Of course," said Wendy.

Peter sighed with relief. "You see, I would feel old if I really were their father."

"But they are our children, yours and mine."

"Not really!"

Wendy took a deep breath and continued. "Peter, what are your feelings toward me?"

"Like that of a noble son," Peter replied solemnly.

"I thought so." Saying this, she went to a far corner of the room.

Peter commented on how strange women were, including Tiger Lily. "She said she wants to become something to me, but not my mother! What is it, then?" wondered Peter aloud.

"A lady doesn't speak of such things," Wendy replied primly.

"Fine. I'll just go ask Tinker Bell," said Peter.

Tinker Bell came out from her room and immediately began being rude to Wendy.

After that, the mood changed. The next hour was filled with dancing and singing. They even

Chapter 9

ended up having pillow fights and they told one another stories before it was time to hear Wendy's good night story.

When Wendy began her story, it was one that the boys loved but Peter hated. Normally when she'd tell this story, he'd go out of the room or he'd cover his ears with his hands. But tonight, he just sat on the stool and watched Wendy tell the Lost Boys her story.

Wendy's Story

Wendy began her story.

"There was once a gentleman—"

"I'd rather there be a lady," said Curly.

"Quiet!" Wendy scolded. "There

was also a lady—"

"Oh, Mummy," cried the first Twin, "you mean that there is a lady also, don't you? She is not dead, is she?"

"Oh, no!"

"I am awfully glad she isn't dead," said Tootles. "Are you glad, John?"

"Of course, I am."

"Are you glad, Nibs?"

"Rather."

"Are you glad, Twins?"

"We are glad."

"Oh dear," sighed Wendy.

"Little less noise here," said Peter, who wanted Wendy to continue with her story.

Wendy took a deep breath and continued. "The gentleman was Mr.

Darling, the lady, Mrs. Darling."

John and Michael quietly said that they knew them.

"They were married, and had three descendents," said Wendy.

"What are descendents?" asked one of the Twins.

"They're children, Twin,"

said John, rolling his eyes in exasperation.

"Now, these threse children had a faithful nurse called Nana, but Mrs. Darling got angry with her one night and chained her to the backyard. That very night, all her children flew away. They flew to Neverland, where the Lost Boys lived," continued Wendy.

"Oh, Wendy," cried Tootles, "was one of the lost children called Tootles?"

"Yes, he was."

"I am in a story. Hurrah, I am in a story, Nibs."

"Hush, think of how unhappy those parents are who've lost their children. Think of all the empty beds and nurseries!" said Wendy.

"If you knew how great a mother's love is," Wendy told the Lost Boys triumphantly, "you would have no fear."

She had now come to the part that Peter hated. "You see, boys, our heroine knew that the mother would always leave the window open for her children to fly back; so the heroine and her brothers stayed back for many happy years."

"Did they ever go back?"

Wendy stood up. "Let us take a look into the future. Behold, who is this elegant lady getting off at London station? Can it be—yes—no—it is—the fair Wendy!"

"Oh!"

"And who are the two noble figures accompanying her, now grown-up men? Can they be John and Michael? Yes, they are!"

"Oh!"

Wendy pointed upward. "Look up there, my brothers. The window is still open. So they all flew to the window into the arms of their mother and father."

That was the end of Wendy's story, and everyone, including the narrator, was pleased with how it turned out. But there was one there who knew better, and when Wendy finished, he uttered a hollow groan.

She ran to Peter, thinking he was ill. "What is it, Peter? Are you in pain?" She rubbed her hand over his stomach.

"It isn't that sort of pain," said Peter. After a while he told Wendy that she was wrong about mothers. He then told all those who were present about his hidden fears, and opinions about mothers.

"Long ago, I thought like you that my mother would keep the window open for me. So I stayed away for a very long time. Then one day, I decided to go back home. So I did, only to find that my mother had forgotten all about me. My window was barred, and I found another boy sleeping in my bed."

"Are you sure mothers are like that?" asked Nibs.

Peter nodded in reply.

John and Michael ran to Wendy. "Wendy, let us go home!" Wendy held both of them in her arms tightly. She murmured her agreement.

"Not tonight!" cried the Lost Boys.

"Immediately!" said Wendy. "Mother must be mourning us." She turned to Peter and asked if he could make all the necessary arrangements.

"If you wish it," he replied, as coolly as if she had asked him to pass the nuts. In truth, he cared that she was leaving very much! He went to his tree, and only returned to the underground home after giving some instructions to the Redskins.

Once there, he saw how bad the situation had become. The Lost Boys, panicked at the thought of losing Wendy, advanced on her and said to themselves that they should hold her. Wendy's first thought was to run. But then, she turned to silly Tootles for help. He turned on the others. "If any of you treats Wendy ungentlemanly, I will hurt him!"

When they saw Peter's expression, they knew that Wendy

had to go. Peter would never hold a girl in Neverland against her will.

He walked up to Wendy. "I've asked the Redskins to guide you through the woods."

"Thank you, Peter."

He continued in a sharp voice, one that is obeyed by all. "Then, Tinker Bell will take her across the

sea. Nibs, go wake her up."

Nibs went and woke up Tinker Bell, who was annoyed at having her sleep disturbed. "Tink, wake up! You have to take Wendy home."

Even though the tiny fairy was thrilled that Wendy was going back, she pretended not to hear a thing.

"Peter, she says no!" cried Nibs.

Peter strode forward and rapped on her bedroom door. "Tink, if you're not up and dressed right now, I shall open the curtains and we'll all see you in your negligee."

This made her leap to the floor. "Who said I wasn't getting up?" she cried.

The boys, in the meantime, helped Wendy and her brothers

prepare for their journey, with sad faces. Wendy took one look at them and told them that if they came with her, her parents would surely adopt them. The invitation, in truth, was meant for Peter only, but the boys jumped around joyously at the thought.

The Lost Boys ran to Peter and asked him if they could go. "All right," Peter replied with a bitter smile, and immediately they rushed to get their things. Just then, Wendy saw a look on his face, one that made her heart sink.

"Peter, go and get your things!" she cried.

"No, I'm not going with you, Wendy," he replied coldly.

To show that he was unaffected by her leaving, he danced around the room, playing his pipes gaily. And so the others had to be told.

"Peter isn't coming."

The boys stopped their activities. Peter not going? They gazed blindly, their bundles tied to a stick and hung on their shoulder.

Peter added darkly that if the boys found mothers, he hoped that they liked them. They didn't know how to react to his behavior.

"Now, then," he said, "no fuss, no crying. Good-bye Wendy!" he said as cheerfully as possible. Wendy walked up to him and asked him gently if he would remember to change their washcloths.

"Yes."

"And you will take your medicine?"

Chapter 10

"Yes."

That being settled, he cried out, "Tink, you ready?"

"Ay, ay."

"Then lead the way."

At that moment, the pirates attacked the Redskins outside. The air outside was filled with the sounds of swords clashing; below there was only silence. Peter picked up his sword, the lust of battle glowing in his eyes.

The Children Are Carried Off

The pirates attacked without any warning, and this everyone understood to be Hook's doing—he was known for his sneak attacks.

The Redskins, in turn, fought with all the glory of their tribe. They were all so alert and sharp, they knew that pirates were near them just by hearing a dry twig crack beneath the pirates' feet. The pirates noticed how the Piccaninnys kept a close guard around the tree in which the Lost Boys were. Hook had no choice but to wait till dawn.

At dawn, twelve of the strongest Redskins stood around the fearless Tiger Lily. They all saw the pirates approaching. Terrible as the sudden appearance of the pirates must have been to them, they remained still for a moment, not a muscle moving.

Then, they seized their weapons and the air was torn with their war cry. Many were killed in the battle between the buccaneers and the braves. But the braves did not die in vain.

The night's work was not yet over, for it was not the Redskins that Hook had come out to destroy. It was Peter he wanted, Peter and Wendy and their band, but mainly

Peter.

The truth was that there was something about Peter that made the pirate captain crazy. It was not his courage; it was not his engaging appearance. It was Peter's smartness. This had got on Hook's nerves; it made his iron claw twitch, and at night it disturbed him like an insect. While Peter lived, Hook felt that he was a lion in a cage into which a sparrow had come.

Suddenly, all the chaos stopped. Which side had won?

The pirates, listening avidly at the holes in the trees, heard the question put by every boy, and alas, they also heard Peter Pan's answer.

"If the Redskins have won," he

said, "they will beat the tom-tom; it is always their sign of victory. Then we can all safely go out."

But Smee had found the tom-tom and was sitting on it. Just then, he saw Hook, who signaled him to play the tom-tom. Twice, Smee beat upon the instrument, and then stopped to listen gleefully.

"The tom-tom," the villains heard Peter cry, "an Indian victory!

Chapter 11

We are safe now!"

This was followed by a deafening cheer. The Lost Boys happily repeated their good-byes to Peter, which thoroughly confused the pirates. But they were happy with the fact that their enemy would soon come out of his tree.

Rapidly and silently Hook gave his orders: one man to each tree, and the others to arrange themselves in a line. After doing so, they gleefully waited for the boys to come out.

Do You Believe
in Fairies?

One by one, all the boys were plucked from their trees in a ruthless manner; and several of them were in the air at a time, like bales of goods flung from hand to hand. With Wendy, however, the treatment was different. With insincere politeness, Hook raised his hat and offered his arm to Wendy as she stepped out of the tree, escorting her to the spot where the others were bound and gagged. She was too shocked at the turn of events to even cry out.

Hook's lip was curled in wicked victory. He indicated that the little house must be used as a conveyance.

The children were flung into it,

four stout pirates raised it on their shoulders, the others fell in behind, and, singing the hateful pirate chorus, the strange procession set off through the woods. As the little house disappeared in the forest, a brave though tiny jet of smoke issued from its chimney as if defying Hook.

The first thing Hook did on finding himself alone in the fast falling night was to tiptoe to Slightly's tree and make sure that it provided him with a passage. He carefully listened for any sound, and got nothing but absolute silence. Was that boy asleep, or did he stand waiting at the foot of Slightly's tree, with his dagger in his hand? The only way to find out was by going down the tree.

Hook removed his hat and entered the tree. He managed to get to the foot of the shaft without getting ambushed. As he stood catching his breath, he looked around the dim room. Once his eyes got accustomed to the lighting, he spotted Peter fast asleep on his bed, and he smiled wickedly.

Peter continued to sleep, unaware of all that had just happened. Thus, he was caught defenseless by Hook, who stood at the foot of the bed and watched Peter sleep. What annoyed Hook was the way in which Peter slept; mouth open, arm drooping, knee arched.

At that moment, Hook noticed Peter's medicine on the table and knew immediately that the boy was at his mercy. He went to the table and took out from his coat pocket a tiny vial carrying a very strong poison, made by Hook himself. He poured five drops of it into Peter's cup. He threw one last glaring look at the sleeping Peter, turned, and made his way up the tree with much difficulty.

Peter slept till ten o'clock. Suddenly he was woken by a soft tapping on the door of his tree. Clutching his dagger, he cried out, "Who is it?"

No answer. In two long strides he walked up to the door and shouted that he wouldn't open it unless he knew who was outside. He heard a voice calling him from outside.

"Peter, it's me. Let me in." It was Tinker Bell. When he opened the door, she flew in excitedly, her face streaked with mud. She quickly told Peter about Wendy and the boys' capture. Peter's blood boiled at the thought of Wendy being bound and gagged on a pirate ship.

"I'll rescue her!"

He then thought that he must first do something to please her. His eyes fell on his medicine cup on the table. He picked up the glass and was about to drink it when Tinker Bell screamed, tugging away at his hand, "No! It's poisoned!"

"Poisoned? Who could have poisoned it?"

"Hook."

"Don't be silly. How could Hook have got down here?"

This, unfortunately, Tinker Bell could not answer, for she didn't know how Hook had got in.

"Besides," said Peter, quite believing himself, "I never fell asleep all this while."

He raised the cup to his lips. Without wasting a second, Tinker Bell flew up to the rim and drank all that was there in the cup, completely emptying it.

"How dare you take my medicine!" Peter shouted.

But she didn't reply, for the poison was already taking effect. She started reeling in the air.

"Tink! What's the matter with

suddenly, for all the mothers must have gone to the nurseries to see why their children were clapping. But that didn't matter, for Tinker Bell was already recovering. First she got her voice back, and then she flew around the room fast, the light glowing strong from her.

"And now to rescue Wendy!"

The moon was hidden by clouds when Peter stepped out of his tree, his weapons strapped around his waist. He was thankful that the moon was covered, for then he could fly without being easily noticed. As he saw the crocodile stealthily pass him, he knew then in his heart that death was just around the bend.

He knew that it would be the end for either him or Hook.

Chapter 12

The Pirate Ship

The *Jolly Roger* was a wicked-looking craft, docked at Kidd's Creek. She was wrapped in the blanket of night. Her frightful reputation preceded her.

There was little sound. A few pirates were leaning over the rails on the deck, to breathe in the night mist, while others busied themselves in games like dice and cards. Smee was at the sewing machine, stitching.

Hook walked the deck, deep

in thought, even though it was his hour of glory. Peter Pan was forever removed from his way because of the poisoned medicine, and the other boys were about to walk the plank. Still, there was no joy in his walk. In fact, he seemed positively dejected. It was because he was so terribly alone.

His mood darkened at the fact that all the children were scared of him, but not of Smee! They found him lovable! The more horrid the things he'd say to them, the more they'd cling on to him. Michael even tried on his spectacles.

The unhappy Hook was as powerless as he was insecure. When his men created a racket, he snapped out of his sadness and stood straight again. He turned to Smee. "Are all the children tied so that they don't fly away?"

"Aye, aye, Captain!" replied Smee.

"Hoist them up," said Hook.

The prisoners were dragged from the hold, except Wendy, who was brought straight to Hook. He said in a loud voice, "Listen up, six of you will walk the plank while two of you become my cabin boys. Who'll it be?"

Now Wendy had already warned the boys back in the hold not to upset Hook. He pointed to John. "You, boy, you look like someone who is to the point. Tell me, did you ever in your heart want to become a pirate?"

John replied after a few

moments, "I once thought of the name Red-Handed Jack."

"That's a good name. We'll call you that, if you join us," said Hook, a glint in his eye.

"What do you think, Michael?" asked John.

"What would I be called if I joined?" asked Michael in a small voice.

"Black-beard Joe."

Michael was impressed and looked imploringly at John, who asked Hook if they'd still serve the king.

Through his teeth, Hook replied, "You'd have to say, 'Down with the king.'"

John and Michael refused at that very instant to join Hook.

"Your fate is sealed. Bring out their mother and ready the plank!" ordered Hook. Being only boys, they got scared looking at Cecco making the plank ready. But when Wendy appeared before them, they put on their

bravest faces.

How Wendy hated the pirates. Hook spoke to her in a sweet voice, "Well, my beauty. Your children are about to walk the plank."

"Are they going to die?" asked Wendy with shock and fear.

"They are. Silence, all of you! Let her share some last words with her children."

Wendy proudly looked at the boys and said the following in an inspirational voice that enthralled even the Pirates:

"These are my last words, dear boys," she said firmly. "I feel that I have a message to you from your real mothers, and it is this: We hope our sons will die like good English gentlemen."

The boys burst out crying and vowed to do what Wendy wanted them to. Once Hook found his voice again, he gave orders to tie Wendy up.

As Smee tied her to the mast, he whispered to her, "I'll let you go, if you promise to be my mother."

"I'd rather have no children at all," said Wendy.

This exchange between Smee and Wendy went unnoticed as all eyes were on the plank and on the boys, ready to take their last steps. As Hook walked toward Wendy to turn her head so that she could watch the boys jump to their fate, he heard a sound that nearly caused his heart to stop beating.

It was the terrible tick-tick of

the crocodile. The sound was heard by all on board. Hook's behavior changed in a second from fearless to fearful.

The sound came steadily nearer; and in advance of it came

Chapter 13

this ghastly thought: "The crocodile is about to board the ship!"

He cried out hoarsely to his men, "Hide me!"

The pirates all gathered around him, knowing in their hearts that his fate was sealed.

The boys rushed to the ship's side out of curiosity to watch the crocodile's climb. What they saw was unbelievable. It wasn't the crocodile—it was Peter! He quickly signaled them to not show signs that they saw him and continued ticking.

"Hook or Me This Time"

Peter was flying silently around the island when he came across the crocodile. He heard the ticking and realized that he could use it to his advantage, knowing Hook's fear of the crocodile. Peter imitated the crocodile's ticking, giving the pirates the impression that he was the crocodile. This is exactly what he hoped for, but he didn't think of one thing: The real crocodile was among those who heard the sound, and it silently followed Peter.

The crocodile! No sooner did Peter remember it, than he heard the ticking. Peter was confused when he heard the sound and looked behind him swiftly. Seeing nothing, Peter reminded himself that he was probably still making the noises to scare the pirates.

"How clever of me!" he thought at once, and signaled to the boys not to burst into applause.

At that moment, the quartermaster emerged on the deck. While Peter stabbed him, John covered his mouth so that his groan could not be heard. As he fell forward, four boys came forward to catch him so that the thud wouldn't be heard. At the signal, the boys threw the man overboard and they heard a splash as the body hit the water.

"One," counted Slightly.

The pirates began moving around, for they didn't hear the ticking. "It's gone, Captain," Smee said, wiping his spectacles.

"All's still again." Hook looked

around and listened carefully for the ticking. When he heard nothing, he drew up to his full height. He hated the boys even more for having seen him break down like this.

The boys quietly looked at one another—they had seen Peter sneak into the pirates' cabin! They then saw Pirate Billy Jukes as he strode to the cabin.

Hook was singing a song when he was cut short by a terrible screech from within the cabin. This was followed by the crowing sound understood by the boys, but which sounded eerie to the pirates.

"Two," said Slightly.

The Italian Cecco hesitated for a moment, and then burst into the cabin. He came staggering out. "What's wrong with Jukes?" hissed Hook.

"He's dead. Stabbed," said Cecco in a hollow voice.

"The cabin's as black as a pit," Cecco said, almost gibbering, "but there is something terrible in there—the thing you heard crowing." Hook noticed the happy excitement of the boys and the scared looks of the pirates.

"Cecco," he said in his most steely voice, "go back and fetch me out that doodle-doo."

Cecco begged not to be sent in, but Hook gave him a dark look. The Italian went inside the cabin, flinging his arms everywhere. There was a moment of silence, followed by a death screech, then silence again. Nobody spoke except Slightly: "Three." Hook turned on his men. "Who's to go in and bring me that doodle-doo?"

"We'll wait till Cecco comes out," growled Starkey, the others supporting him.

"I think I heard you volunteer, Starkey," said Hook, purring again.

"Not likely!" cried Starkey.

"My sharp hook thinks you did," said Hook, going toward to him. "Starkey, don't you think you should obey the hook?"

When he looked behind him, Starkey saw no forthcoming support. He saw the hard glint in Hook's eyes, turned, and threw himself overboard.

"Four," counted Slightly.

Seizing a lantern and waving his hook around in a menacing fashion, Hook said, "I'll bring the doodle-doo out myself!"

Slightly was ready to say "Five" but didn't, for Hook came staggering out.

"Something blew out the light," he said unsteadily.

"What of Cecco?" asked Noodler.

"He's dead, just like Jukes."

All pirates are superstitious, and Cookson cried, "They do say the surest sign of a ship's doom is when there's one on board more than can be accounted for."

Hook had forgotten about his prisoners, but at that moment he

saw them and smiled. "Lads," he shouted, "let them fight the doodle-doo for their lives. If they kill the beast inside the cabin, we're so much the better; if they get killed, we're none the worse."

The boys pretended to struggle

as they were pushed inside the cabin, the pirates locking the door behind them.

All this time, Wendy was tied to the mast; but she didn't have to wait any longer. In the cabin, Peter found the key that unlocked the boys' chains. After freeing them and signaling them to hide, he rushed to Wendy and cut her bonds. They all could have easily flown away, but there was just one thought that prevented Peter from doing so. "Hook or me this time."

He told her to hide herself with the others, taking her place at the mast. He wrapped himself in her cloak.

"Fling the girl overboard," cried

Hook, and they made a rush at the figure in the cloak.

"There's no one who can save you now, missy," Pirate Mullins hissed jeeringly.

"There's one," replied the figure.

"Who's that?"

"Peter Pan!" came the terrible answer, and as he spoke, Peter flung off his cloak. Then they all knew who it was who had been undoing them in the cabin. Twice, Hook tried to speak and twice, he failed. Peter Pan was still alive!

At last he cried, "Cleave him to the brisket!" But it was without conviction.

At that moment, Peter gave orders to the boys to attack. In a moment, the sound of weapons clashing vibrated through the ship.

As the pirates were not prepared, it was easier for the boys to overpower them. Some of the miscreants leaped into the sea;

others hid in dark recesses, where they were found by Slightly, who did not fight. Instead, he ran about with a lantern that he flashed in their faces so that they were half blinded and fell as an easy prey to the reeking swords of the other boys.

There was little sound to be heard but the clang of weapons, an occasional screech or splash, and Slightly counting away—five—six—seven—eight—nine—ten—eleven.

Suddenly, in the middle of the noise, Hook found himself face-to-face with Peter Pan.

The others drew back and formed a ring around them. The two occupants in the ring stared at each other for a long time.

"So, Pan," said Hook at last,

"this is all your doing."

"Ay, James Hook," came the stern answer, "it is all my doing."

"Proud and rude youth," said Hook, "prepare to meet your death."

"Dark and sinister man," Peter answered, "prepare to die, too."

With that, they charged at each other. Peter was a superb swordsman.

Hook was quite good himself, but to his surprise, he found his thrusts turned aside all the time. Peter then lunged fiercely and pierced him in the ribs.

At the sight of his own blood, Hook dropped his sword, thus being at Peter's mercy. "Now!" cried all the boys, but with a magnificent gesture, Peter invited his opponent to pick up his sword. Hook did so instantly, but with a tragic feeling that Peter was showing good form.

"Pan, who and what are you?" he cried huskily.

"I'm youth, I'm joy," Peter answered at a venture, "I'm a little bird that has broken out of the egg."

Abandoning the fight, Hook rushed to a barrel of gun powder and lit it.

"In two minutes," he cried, "the ship will be blown to pieces."

However, Peter calmly picked up the barrel of gun powder in his hands and flung it overboard.

Seeing Peter slowly advancing upon him through the air with dagger poised, Hook got ready to jump into the sea and swim away. He did not know that the crocodile was waiting for him.

As he stood on the edge, looking over his shoulder at Peter gliding through the air, he invited him with a gesture to use his foot. It made Peter kick instead of stab.

Hook fell straight into the crocodile's mouth.

That was the end of Captain James Hook.

Wendy, of course, had stood by, taking no part in the fight, though watching Peter with glistening eyes. Now that all was over, she became prominent again. She praised all the boys equally.

Chapter 14

The Return Home

The next morning, the boys dressed up like pirates, and Tootles was among them, with a rope's end in his hand and chewing tobacco. It is quite obvious who the ship's captain was.

Nibs and John were first and second mate. There was a woman on board. The rest were sailors running around doing odd jobs on the deck. Peter took hold of the wheel. Then a few sharp orders were given, and they turned the ship around and nosed her for the mainland.

Wendy, John, and Michael had been planning their return for weeks. They also thought of the reactions they'd get when they returned; Mother's rapture, Father's shout of joy, and Nana's leap through the air to embrace them first.

Back in London, in the Darling home, the only change to be seen in the night-nursery was that between nine and six, Nana's kennel was no longer there. When the children flew away, Mr. Darling

hin two
d flying
hisper is
Let's try!
she has
names;
the room

my dear
Nana went
tly put her
was how
m when he

und inside
his wife if
ho so that he
if she could
r a cold draft

felt that all the blame was his for having chained Nana up, and that from the beginning she had been wiser than he. Having thought the matter out with anxious care after the flight of the children, he went down on all fours and crawled into

the kennel. To all

dear invitations to

he replied sadly bu

dearest, this is the

In the bitter

remorse he swore t

never leave the ken

children came back

this was a pity. B

Mr. Darling did, he h

excess; otherwise, he s

doing it.

Every morning, t

was carried with Mr. Da

to a cab, which conveyed

office, and he returned ho

same way at six.

The day the childre

back home, Mrs. Darlin

sadness in her eyes, was wa

back? They are really wit

miles of the window now, a

strong, but all we need w

that they are on the way.

It is a pity we did it, for

started up, calling thei

and there was no one in

but Nana.

"O Nana, I dreamt

ones had come back." N

to her mistress and gen

paws on her lap. This

Mr. Darling found the

returned home.

As he curled ar

the tunnel, he asked

she could play the pia

could sleep, and also

close the windows, fo

was blowing in.

"Never ask me to do that, George. The window must always remain open for them to return," said Mrs. Darling. Now it was his turn to beg her pardon; and she went into the day-nursery, and soon he was asleep. While he slept, Peter Pan and Tinker Bell flew into the room.

"Quick, Tink," Peter Pan whispered, "close the window, bar

it. Good. Now you and I must leave by the door. When Wendy arrives and sees the window barred, she'll think her mother has done it. Then she'll have to come back with me."

Peter had planned this all along. He could have easily told Tinker Bell to escort the children back home. Instead of feeling bad, he danced around the room with glee. Just then he heard the sound of the piano. He peeped into the day-nursery to see who was playing it. He whispered to Tinker Bell, "It's Wendy's mother! She is a pretty lady, but not so pretty as my mother. Her mouth is full of thimbles, but not so full as my mother's was."

Of course he knew nothing

about his mother, but he sometimes bragged about her. He did not know the tune she played, but he did know that she was saying, "Wendy, come back!"

"Hah! You will never see Wendy again, lady. The window is barred!"

He peeped in again to see why the music had stopped, and now he saw that Mrs. Darling had laid her head on the box and that two tears were sitting in her eyes.

"She wants me to unbar the window," thought Peter, "but I won't, not I!" He peeped again, and the tears were still there, or another two had taken their place.

"She's awfully fond of Wendy," he said to himself. He was angry with her now for not seeing why she could not have Wendy back.

The reason was so simple. "I'm fond of her, too. We can't both have her, lady."

These were a few stressful moments for him. "Oh, all right," he said at last, and gulped. Then he unbarred the window. "Come on, Tink," he cried, with a frightful sneer at the laws of nature, "we don't want any silly mothers." With that, he flew away.

Thus, Wendy, John, and Michael found the window open for them, after all, which of course was more than they deserved. They alighted on the floor, quite unashamed of themselves, and the youngest one had already forgotten his home.

"John," he said, looking around

him doubtfully, "I think I have been here before."

"Of course, you have, you silly. There is your old bed. Look! The kennel." He ran to it and peeped inside. "There's a man inside."

"It's father!" exclaimed Wendy.

"Let me see Father," Michael begged eagerly, and he took a good look. "He is not as big as the pirate I killed," he said with frank disappointment.

Wendy and John were surprised to find their father in the kennel. "It's shameful of Mother," said John, "not to be here when we got back."

Just then, they heard the piano. "It's Mother!" they cried.

"Let us creep in," John suggested, "and put our hands

over her eyes." But Wendy had a better idea. And so, when Mrs. Darling went back to the night-nursery to see if her husband was asleep, all the beds were occupied.

The children waited for her cry of joy, but it didn't come. She saw them so often in their beds in her dreams that when she saw them for real, she thought she was dreaming again.

The children could not understand this, and a cold fear set on them as they watched their mother sit down on her chair in the nursery.

"Mother" Wendy cried.

"That's Wendy," Mrs. Darling said, but still, she was sure it was the dream.

"Mother!"

"That's John," she said.

"Mother!" cried Michael. He knew her now.

"That's Michael," she said, now really seeing the three selfish children, and she stretched out her arms for them.

"George, the children are back!" she cried, when she could speak again. Mr. Darling woke up and shared her bliss, while Nana came running in to see what all the noise was about.

It was such a lovely sight, and nobody saw it except one boy who was staring in at the family. He was looking at the one joy from which he must be forever barred.

Chapter 15

When Wendy Grew Up

Wile Wendy and her brothers reconciled with their parents, the Lost Boys were nervously waiting below, giving Wendy time to explain to her parents. They counted to 500 slowly, and then went upstairs. They thought this would make a better pression than flying in.

They stood in a row in front of Mrs. Darling, with their hats off and wishing they were not wearing their pirate clothes. They said nothing, but their eyes asked her to have them.

Of course, Mrs. Darling said at once that she would have them; but Mr. Darling was curiously depressed, and they saw that he considered six a rather large number to look

after.

"George!" Mrs. Darling exclaimed, pained to see her husband showing himself in such an unfavorable light. Then he burst into tears, and the truth came out. He was as glad to have them as she was, he said, but he thought they should have asked his consent as well as hers, instead of treating him as someone unimportant in his own house.

"I don't think you're unimportant," said Tootles. "Do you, Curly?"

"Not in the least. Slightly?" asked Curly.

"Not me. What about you, Twins?"

"We don't either."

Mr. Darling was absurdly gratified, and said he would find space for them all in the drawing room if they fitted in. They assured him that they would.

As for Peter, he saw Wendy once again before he flew away. He did not exactly come to the window, but he brushed against it in passing so that she could open it if she liked and call to him. That is just what she did.

"Hullo, Wendy, good-bye," he said.

"Oh dear, are you going away?"

"Yes."

Mrs. Darling came to the window, for at present she was keeping a sharp eye on Wendy. She told Peter that she had adopted all the other boys, and would like to adopt him also.

"Would you send me to school?" he inquired craftily.

"Yes."

"And then to an office?"

"I suppose so."

"Soon I would be a man?"

"Very soon."

But Peter refused all that she offered him.

"But where are you going to live?" Mrs. Darling asked.

"With Tink, high up among the treetops, I'll have so much fun," he said cheerfully.

"It will be so lonely in the evenings, sitting by the fire," sighed Wendy.

"Well, then, come with me to the little house."

"May I, Mummy?" Wendy asked her mother.

"Certainly not. I have got you home again, and I mean to keep you here."

"But he does so need a mother."

"So do you, my love."

"Oh, all right." Peter said, as if he had asked her from politeness merely. But Mrs. Darling saw his mouth twitch, and she made this lovely offer: to let Wendy go to him for a week every year to do his spring cleaning.

Wendy would have preferred a more permanent arrangement, and it seemed to her that spring would be long in coming; but this promise sent Peter away quite happy again.

The Lost Boys went to school. The more they stayed back, the more the power to fly lessened in them. Michael believed longer than the others, earning a lot of jeers rom the boys. He was with Wendy when Peter came for her at the end of the first year.

Wendy was pained to find that the past year was but as yesterday to Peter; it had seemed such a long year of waiting, to her. But he was exactly as fascinating as ever, and they had a lovely spring cleaning in the little house in the treetops.

Next year he did not come for her. She waited in a new frock because the old one didn't fit anymore, but he never came.

When Peter came next spring cleaning, he never knew he had missed a year. That was the last time Wendy as a girl saw him.

The years rolled by, and when they met again, Wendy was all

grown up and married. All the boys had grown up, too.

The Twins, Nibs, and Curly went to an office each day. Michael was an engine driver. Slightly had married a lady with a title, becoming Lord Slightly. Tootles became a judge, while John became a bearded man who didn't have a story to tell his children.

Years rolled by, and Wendy had a daughter named Jane. She loved to hear of Peter, and Wendy told her all she could remember in the very nursery from which the famous flight had taken place.

It was Jane's nursery now, for her father had bought it from Wendy's father, who was no longer fond of stairs.

Mrs. Darling was now dead and forgotten. Poor old Nana had also passed away with old age. There were only two beds in the nursery now-one belonged to Jane and the other to her nurse.

The nurse had day off once a week. Those days, Wendy put her daughter to bed and told her all her wonderful stories.

"That is a long time ago, sweetheart," said Wendy. "Oh my, how time flies!"

"Does it fly," asked the child, "the way you flew when you were a little girl?"

"The way I flew? Do you know, Jane, I sometimes wonder whether I ever did really fly."

"Yes, you did."

"The dear old days when I could fly!"

"Why can't you fly now, Mother?"

"Because I am grown up, dearest. When people grow up, they forget the way."

"Why do they forget the way?"

"Because they are no longer happy and innocent. It is only the happy and innocent who can fly."

Wendy was now talking about the great adventure of the night when Peter flew in looking for his shadow.

"And then he flew us all away to the Neverland and the fairies and the pirates and the Redskins and the mermaid's lagoon and the home under the ground," she said with a faraway look in her eyes.

"What was the last thing Peter ever said to you?"

"The last thing he ever said to me was, 'Just always be waiting for me, and then some night you will hear me crowing.'"

"What did his crow sound like?" Jane asked one evening.

"It was like this," Wendy said, trying to imitate Peter's crow.

"No, it wasn't," Jane said gravely. "It was like this—" and she did it ever so much better than her Mother.

Wendy was a little startled. "My darling, how can you know?"

"I often hear it when I am sleeping," Jane said.

One night by sheer surprise, Peter dropped in on Wendy while she was sleeping in the nursery. He was exactly the same as ever, and Wendy saw at once that he still had all his first teeth.

He greeted her as if she hadn't changed at all.

"Where's John?"

"He's not here."

"Is Michael asleep?" he asked, looking at the bed where Jane slept.

"Yes, I suppose so." She saw Peter looking at the bed. "That isn't Michael asleep in the bed."

"Oh, a new one. Boy or girl?"

"Girl. Peter, are you expecting me to fly away with you?"

"Of course. That's why I've come for you. Have you forgotten about the spring cleaning?" he added a bit sternly.

"I can't come, I've forgotten how to fly," she said apologetically.

"Not a problem. I'll teach you again."

"Peter, don't."

Suddenly Peter realized that something was wrong. "What's the matter?"

Wendy took a deep breath and switched on the lights. When Peter saw her, he gave a cry of pain. When the tall, beautiful creature came to him, he shrank back.

"I've grown-up, Peter. I grew up a long time ago. I'm more than twenty years old."

"But you promised not to!" cried Peter.

"I had no choice. I'm a married

woman now. The girl sleeping there, she's my daughter. Her name is Jane."

Peter went to the foot of Jane's bed and started crying. Wendy ran out of the room to think. Peter's sobs woke Jane up.

"Boy, why are you crying?" she asked softly.

Peter stopped crying instantly and bowed to her. She bowed from her bed.

"I'm Peter Pan."

"Yes, I know," replied Jane.

"I've come here for my mother, to take her back to Neverland with me."

"Yes, I know," Jane said. "I have been waiting for you."

When Wendy returned to the

room, she found Peter sitting on the bedpost crowing gloriously, while Jane in her nighty was flying round the room in solemn ecstasy.

"Good-bye" said Peter to Wendy, and he rose in the air. Jane rose with him, too.

Wendy rushed to the window.

"No, no," she cried, trying to stop Jane.

"It is just for spring cleaning time," Jane said. "He wants me always to do his spring cleaning."

"If only I could go with you," Wendy sighed.

"You can't fly," said Jane.

Of course, in the end, Wendy let them fly away together.

Many years rolled by. Wendy had become an old lady, with snow white hair.

Her daughter Jane was now a married woman, with her own daughter, Margaret.

Every spring cleaning time, except when he forgot, Peter came for Margaret. He took her to the Neverland, where she told him stories about himself, to which he listened eagerly.

When Margaret grows up she will have a daughter, who is to be Peter's mother in turn; and thus it will go on, so long as children are happy and innocent.

About the Author

Sir James Matthew Barrie (May 9, 1860 - June 19, 1937) was more commonly known as J. M. Barrie. He was a Scottish novelist and dramatist and is best remembered for creating *Peter Pan* or *The Boy Who Would Not Grow Up*.

When Barrie was six years old, his brother David died in a skating accident. His mother never recovered from this loss and ignored young Barrie. The mother found comfort in the fact that her dead son would remain a boy forever—he would never grow up and leave her. This was probably the author's inspiration for this story.